# Mo

## Who (

## Scare

De

Illustrated l

Hippo

Scholastic Children's Books,
Scholastic Publications Ltd,
7-9 Pratt Street, London NW1 OAE, UK

Scholastic Inc.,
555 Broadway, New York, NY 10012-3999, USA

Scholastic Canada Ltd,
123 Newkirk Road, Richmond Hill,
Ontario, Canada L4C 3G5

Ashton Scholastic Pty Ltd,
PO Box 579, Gosford, New South Wales,
Australia

Ashton Scholastic Ltd,
Private Bag 92801, Penrose, Auckland,
New Zealand

First published by Scholastic Children's Books, 1994
Text copyright © Denis Bond, 1994
Illustrations copyright © Valeria Petrone, 1994

ISBN O 590 55717 3

Typeset by Rapid Reprographics
Printed by Proost International Book Production

In the dusty bedroom of a large, empty house stood an old, iron bed. Under the old, iron bed there lived a monster. He was a very unhappy monster. He had nobody to scare.

During the day, he would stomp around the large, empty house making monster noises. "YUGGA! YUGGA!" But all the rooms were empty. There was no one to scare.

At night he would stomp through the weed-tangled garden, making eerie sounds.
"YUGGA...OOO! YUGGA...OOO!"
The owls and the bats took no notice. They weren't scared of monsters.

One moonlit night, when an owl screeched, "WHOO! WHOO!" the monster ran to hide behind a large oak tree. He trembled from the top of his head to the tips of his toes. He was scared of owls!

Then...FLAP! FLAP! FLAP! a bat
swept over the monster's head.
The monster screamed and ran back
to the large, empty house. He was
scared of bats.

Next morning, the monster stared sadly through the dirty windows of the large, empty house. Then he saw a lorry pull up outside. People began unloading huge crates...and furniture...and curtains...and lots and lots of toys.

Later that day, as he peered over the banisters from the top landing, the monster spied a dad, a mum, a granny and a small boy. They were putting down rugs and filling the sitting-room with furniture.

"At last!" cried the monster.
"Someone to scare!"
And he raced down the stairs,
crying, "YUGGA! YUGGA!"
"Look, everyone!" yelled the small
boy. "A monster!"
"Go away, monster," tutted Granny.
"Can't you see we're busy?"

That evening the monster crept up behind Mum and Dad, who were sitting on the sofa, watching the television.

"YUGGA! YUGGA!" he cried.

"Come and watch this programme," said Mum. "It's very funny." The monster sat between Mum and Dad and watched the television. Mum and Dad laughed and laughed at the programme. But the monster didn't find it funny at all.

The programme was all about monsters who were scaring people. "What's so funny about *that*," grumbled the monster, as he slunk off to bed.

But the monster's old, iron bed had been removed, so he made his new home under the little boy's bed. During the night, the little boy woke up and began playing with his computer game under the bedclothes.

The monster slid out from under the
bed and stood and stared.
"YUGGA! YUGGA!" he growled.
Startled, the boy leapt from his bed,
with a sheet still over his head.
The monster fled screaming,
"HELP! HELP! There's a ghost in
that room!"

Early next morning, the monster plodded off to the kitchen to see if there was anything for breakfast. Granny was mopping the kitchen floor.

Granny was so busy, she didn't see the monster standing there. "YUGGA! YUGGA!" he shrieked. "AARGH!" screamed Granny, as she leapt into the air. Her wet mop landed on the monster's head, covering him in soapsuds.

Granny fell, bottom first, into her
bucket, as the soapy water sloshed
all over the kitchen floor.
Granny was furious.
Her very wet bottom was stuck in
the bucket.

Mum and Dad ran to help Granny. As they struggled to pull the bucket from Granny's bottom, the monster crept away, feeling very ashamed. He'd made Granny jump...but she wasn't *scared* of him.

Later, Dad decided to dig the weed-tangled garden. He dug deep into the ground and scooped out a shovelful of mud. *Someone* was watching him!

The monster rushed up behind Dad.
He was about to shout, "YUGGA!
YUGGA!" when Dad threw the mud
over his shoulder.
The mud hit the monster, "SPLAT!"
covering him from head to toe.
"Whoops! Sorry!" laughed Dad.

As the mud-splattered, tearful monster sat under the small boy's bed, Granny handed him a glass of milk and a piece of chocolate cake. "Here," she said, kindly. "Your lunch." The monster was surprised.

Granny, Mum and Dad and the small boy felt sorry for the monster who couldn't scare anyone. They decided to make him one of the family. They decorated the inside of the cupboard under the stairs and gave him his own room.

Wherever the family went, the
monster went too. One day they
took him on a train ride into town.
The carriage was full and there was
no seat for the monster.
But he didn't mind. He sat in the
luggage rack.

They took him to a toy-shop.
All the children pointed and stared.
"Look," they giggled. "A monster!"
None of them was scared. But *the
monster* was scared!
He didn't like the toy dragon.

They took him to see a film about
some witches.
Everyone loved the film.
But the monster thought it was far
too scary.

They even took him to a restaurant where they ate spaghetti. But as the tomato sauce dribbled down the monster's chin, he said, "This is very nice, but it must *stop*. I have to scare people. That's my job!"

So that night the monster hurtled around the kitchen rattling pots and pans. He slammed cupboard doors. And he bashed himself on the head with the lid from a biscuit tin. "That'll scare them!" he said.

But Mum and Dad
were sound asleep.

The little boy was
sound asleep.

And Granny was
sound asleep...and
snoring loudly.

Nobody had heard the monster.
He hadn't scared any of them.

The monster hurried into the sitting-room to see what else he could rattle and bang and bash.
But he got a terrible shock!
Someone was loading a big sack with all the family's belongings.
It was a burglar!
The monster was very, very angry.

"YUGGA! YUGGA!" he shouted.
The terrified burglar screamed,
"A MONSTER! HELP!" He dropped his
sack and scrambled through the window.
The monster was very happy.
"I *can* do it!" he said, proudly.

The monster quietly closed the window
and tiptoed around the
room, putting back all the
belongings. He decided not to tell
the family about the burglar.
After all, he didn't want to *scare* them.